Slow Lizard makes room for the feelings of others in a calm, gentle way.
And friends help Slow Lizard too.
It's nice to have friends like these.
Everyone can make someone happy in their very own way.
Maybe today I'll have a fragrant cup of flower tea with a friend, just like Slow Lizard.

—Yeorim Yoon

I enjoy writing and illustrating picture books in my little office every day.
It takes a long time to write and illustrate a book, but spending time this way makes me happy.
Let me tell you a secret: tiny animal friends are hiding throughout these pages.
Can you spot a ladybug, a snail, and a mole? Can you find any others?
Take your time looking at each page and say hi to your new friends.

—Jian Kim

Text © 2019 Yeorim Yoon
Illustrations © 2019 Jian Kim
Originally published in Korea as 괜찮아, 천천히 도마뱀
It's OK, Slow Lizard
Copyright © Woongjin Thinkbig Co., Ltd

English translation rights arranged with Woongjin Thinkbig Co., Ltd
through S.B.Rights Agency – Stephanie Barrouillet

Translation copyright © 2020 Chi-Young Kim
All rights reserved.

No part of this book may be reproduced or transmitted
without the prior written permission of the publisher.

First Restless Books hardcover edition September 2021

Hardcover ISBN: 9781632062772
Library of Congress Control Number: 2021937474

This book is supported in part by an award
from the National Endowment for the Arts.

This book is made possible by the New York State
Council on the Arts with the support of Governor
Andrew M. Cuomo and the New York State Legislature.

Cover design by Jonathan Yamakami
Cover illustration by Jian Kim

Printed in Italy
1 3 5 7 9 10 8 6 4 2

Restless Books, Inc.
232 3rd Street, Suite A101
Brooklyn, NY 11215

www.restlessbooks.org
publisher@restlessbooks.org

IT'S OK, SLOW LIZARD

Yeorim Yoon & Jian Kim

Translated from the Korean by
Chi-Young Kim

Want to relax and listen to my story?

Restless Books
Brooklyn, New York

In the forest,
where sunlight falls gently through the leaves,
live busy Little Bird,
mighty Elephant,
speedy Rabbit,
funny Monkey—
and me, Slow Lizard.

Just like my name,
I live a slow, slow life.
And because I live a slow life,
I see many things,
I hear many things,
and I have lots of time to help my friends.

"Today I need to finish everything
for tomorrow and for the next day.
But when will I have time to do everything
for the day after that?"

When Little Bird,
who does everything early, is anxious—

"Hey, Little Bird,
want to have some flower tea with me?"

As we sip our flower tea,
Little Bird's stress slowly melts away.

When mighty Elephant
gets frustrated and angry—

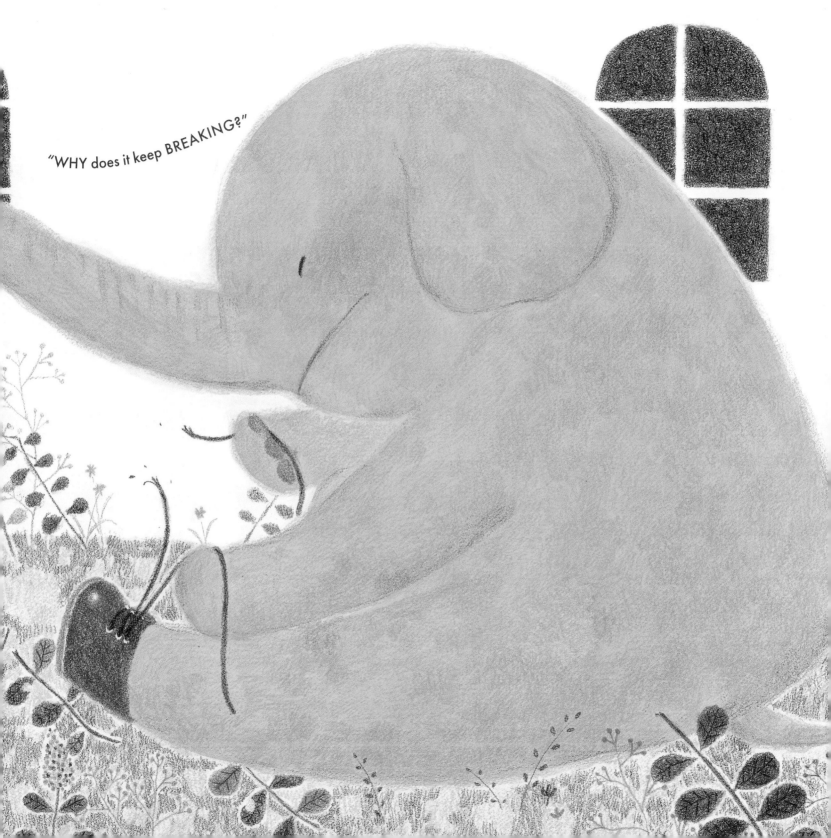

"WHY does it keep BREAKING?"

"Hey, Elephant, want to look at the sky
through the hole in this leaf?
I can tie your shoes for you."

As we look through the hole in the leaf
at the clouds drifting by,
Elephant's anger slowly melts away.

When speedy Rabbit rushes ahead
and (oops!) loses the race by mistake—

I sit quietly next to Rabbit.
With a friend nearby,
Rabbit slowly feels better.

"It's OK to make mistakes.
It's OK to not win."

"Ahh!"

When funny Monkey giggles
and plays pranks on us—

"Ow!"

"Hey, Monkey, want to read this book together?
It's really good."

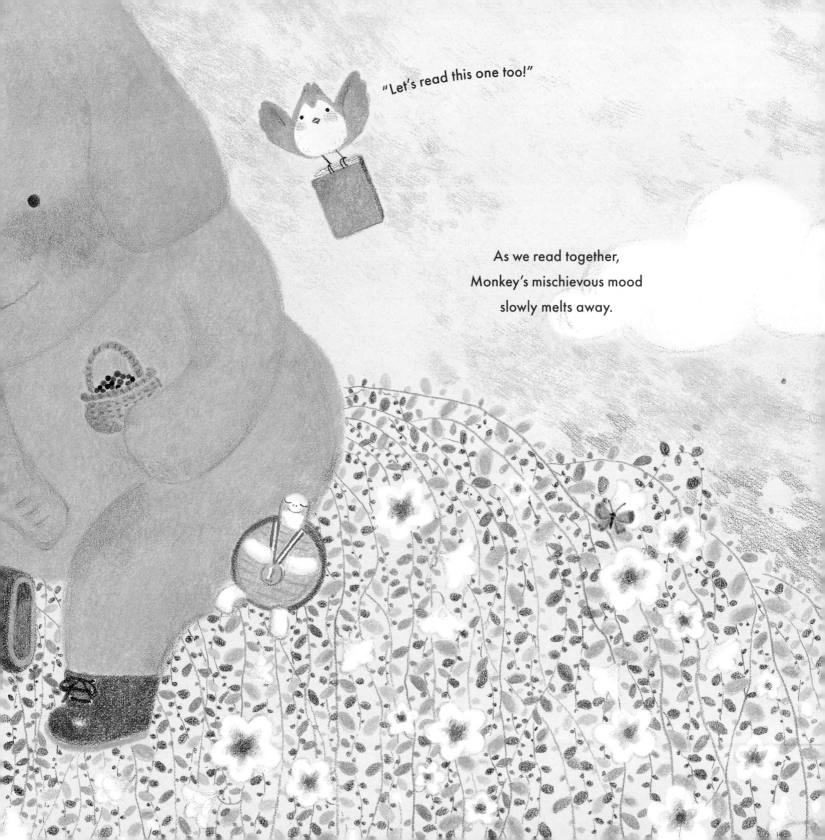

"Let's read this one too!"

As we read together,
Monkey's mischievous mood
slowly melts away.

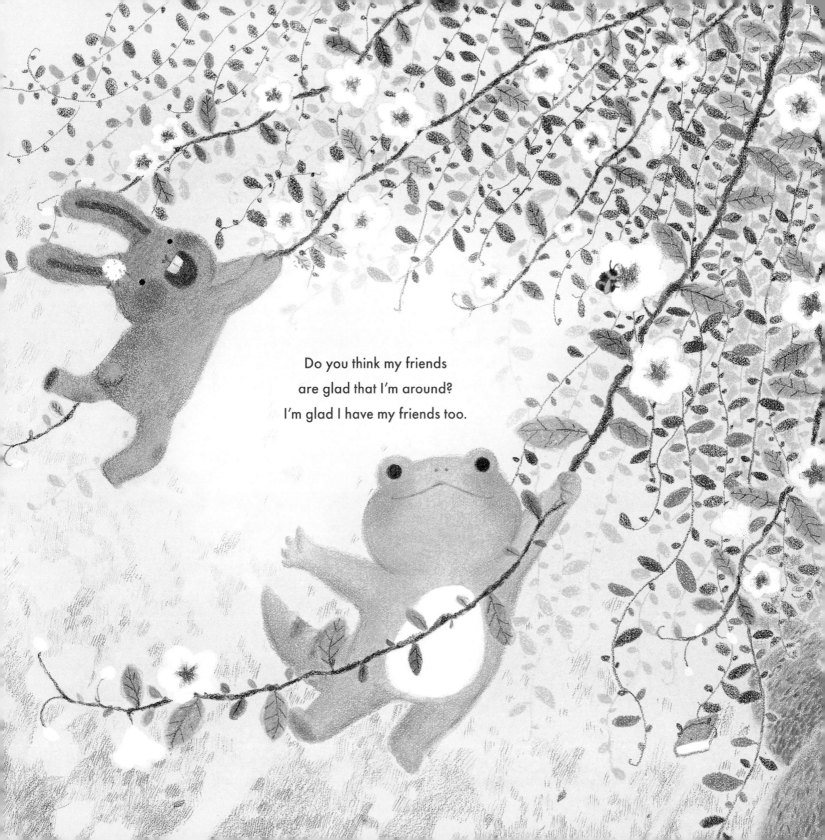

Do you think my friends
are glad that I'm around?
I'm glad I have my friends too.

"It's going to rain tonight,
with thunder and lightning!
Let's pick apples now."

Little Bird is always prepared.

"The apples are heavy, aren't they?
I can give you a ride home."

Elephant is so generous.

"The sun is about to set.
Follow me, I know a shortcut!
We'll get home faster."

Rabbit is really clever.

"Are you afraid of the dark?
I can make you laugh."

Thank goodness for funny Monkey.

"Here we are, safe and sound."

Raindrops start falling slowly
among the leaves.

Even if it's stormy for a while, it's OK.
The rain will always stop
and the sky will always clear up.

Hey, friends,
want to come over
and eat apples?
Take your umbrella,
and take your time.

ABOUT THE AUTHOR

Yeorim Yoon is from Ulsan, South Korea. She is a former editor of children's books at various publishers as well as at the Samsung Children's Museum in Seoul. She currently lives in San Diego, where she leads a life that is both busy and slow as a mother and author of children's books.

ABOUT THE ILLUSTRATOR

Jian Kim is an artist and illustrator of children's books from Seoul, South Korea. She studied animation in college and became interested in picture books after encountering the work of Anthony Browne. She lives in Incheon.

ABOUT THE TRANSLATOR

Chi-Young Kim is an award-winning literary translator and editor based in Los Angeles. A recipient of the Man Asian Literary Prize (2011), she has translated more than a dozen books, including works by Kyung-sook Shin, You-Jeong Jeong, Young-ha Kim, and Ae-ran Kim.

ABOUT YONDER

Yonder is an imprint from Restless Books devoted to bringing the wealth of great stories from around the globe to English-reading children, middle graders, and young adults. Books from other countries, cultures, viewpoints, and storytelling traditions can open up a universe of possibility, and the wider our view, the more powerfully books enrich and expand us. In an increasingly complex, globalized world, stories are potent vehicles of empathy. We believe it is essential to teach our kids to place themselves in the shoes of others beyond their communities, and instill in them a lifelong curiosity about the world and their place in it. Through publishing a diverse array of transporting stories, Yonder nurtures the next generation of savvy global citizens and lifelong readers.